SCARY TALES RETOLD

MW01068067

THE PRINCESS AND THE POISON PEA

by Wiley Blevins • illustrated by Steve Cox

RED CHAIR
•PRESS•

Please visit our website at **www.redchairpress.com** for more high-quality products for young readers.

About the Author

Wiley Blevins has taught elementary school in both the United States and South America. He has also written over 70 books for children and 15 for teachers, as well as created reading programs for schools in the U.S. and Asia with Scholastic, Macmillan/McGraw-Hill, Houghton Mifflin Harcourt, and other publishers. Wiley currently lives and writes in New York City.

About the Artist

Steve Cox lives in Bath, England. He first designed toys and packaging for other people's characters. But he decided to create his own characters and turned full time to illustrating. When he is not drawing books he plays lead guitar in a rock band.

Publisher's Cataloging-In-Publication Data

Names: Blevins, Wiley. | Cox, Steve, 1961- illustrator. | Based on (work): Andersen, H. C. (Hans Christian), 1805-1875. Prindsessen paa aerten. English. | Blevins, Wiley. Scary tales retold.

Title: The princess and the poison pea / by Wiley Blevins ; illustrated by Steve Cox.
Other Titles: Princess and the pea

Description: South Egremont, MA : Red Chair Press, [2017] | Interest age level: 006-009. | Summary: "The King and evil Queen are looking for a proper Princess to marry their Prince. When a Princess is found, will they all live happily ever after? Or will they live at all?"-- Provided by publisher.

Identifiers: LCCN 2016934120 | ISBN 978-1-63440-166-1 (library hardcover) | ISBN 978-1-63440-170-8 (paperback) | ISBN 978-1-63440-174-6 (ebook)

Subjects: LCSH: Princesses--Juvenile fiction. | Poisoning--Juvenile fiction. | Horror tales. | CYAC: Princesses--Fiction. | Poisoning--Fiction. | LCGFT: Fairy tales.

Classification: LCC PZ7.B618652 Pr 2017 (print) | LCC PZ7.B618652 (ebook) | DDC [E]--dc23

Scary Tales Retold first published by:
Red Chair Press LLC   PO Box 333   South Egremont, MA 01258-0333

Printed in the United States of America

0617 1P CGBF17

Once upon a spooky time, a king and queen ruled a small kingdom. Their castle stood at the edge of the dark forest.

The king and queen had only one son. "It is time
for you to marry," said the king to his son.
"We must find you a real princess," said the queen.

All the king's knights jumped on their
horses. They raced through the kingdom
and beyond. "The prince is looking for his
princess," they shouted.

Soon, girls from lands far and wide
arrived at the castle.

"Pick me. Pick me!" they shouted.

"Not so fast," said the king.

"You must prove that you are a real princess," warned the queen. Chills ran down the girls' spines. Many dashed away. The queen took the girls that remained to special rooms in the castle.

Each room had a princess-size bed. On each bed was a stack of ten large mattresses. Underneath the ten large mattresses, the queen placed a tiny pea. But these were no ordinary peas. These peas were *poison*.

"If you are not a real princess," the queen whispered to herself, you will die by morning."

The queen tucked in all the girls and turned out the lights. "Pleasant dreams," she cackled.

The next morning, a pile of bones lay on each bed.
"I knew these girls weren't real princesses," laughed the queen.

Week after week, girl after girl came to the castle. And every morning, the king and queen were greeted with another pile of bones.

The prince didn't care. He only wanted the
most beautiful and real princess in the land
to be his bride. "Silly girls," he said. "You
can't trick us."

One cold and stormy night, the prince heard
a knock on the castle door. "Who would
come here this late?" he asked. Slowly, he
opened the large, creaky door.

There stood a skinny girl dressed in rags. Her clothes were soaked. Her hair dripped and drooped around her face.

"Who are you?" sneered the prince.

"I am the only <u>real</u> princess in the land," said the girl. "My kingdom was stolen from my family years ago. Now I live in a hut in the dark forest."

The queen swooped in to see the girl. "She's a fake," she scowled. "Send her to bed. At least we'll only have a small bag of bones to collect in the morning."

The prince took the girl to a room and locked the door. But the girl was clever. She spotted the pea under the mattresses and carefully slipped it into her bag. Then she crawled into bed and fell asleep.

Everyone was shocked to see the girl alive
the next morning.
"How can this be?" asked the king.
"She can't be a *real* princess," snickered
the queen.
"I won't marry her," cried the prince.

The girl only smiled.

"Thank you for the good night's sleep," she said.

"Let me make you a breakfast feast."

The girl hurried to the kitchen. She grabbed a
big pot and tasty ingredients. Then she added
something special to the bubbling mixture.

"That smells wonderful," said the king.

"What is it?" asked the queen.

"It's a secret recipe," said the girl.

The king and queen grabbed their spoons and slurped it down.

"I hope you enjoyed my special pea soup," hissed the girl.

And minutes later...

The king and queen turned into a pile of bones.

"That will teach you to steal my father's kingdom," said the girl. "I promised I would get it back someday!"

So what happened to the prince?
The princess let him stay in the castle.
And she gave him a very *special* job.

She made him her Royal Toilet Cleaner.
And nothing could be more real!

THE END